For Honey

by Bonnie Highsmith Taylor

Cover Illustration: Dea Marks
Inside Illustration: Dea Marks

For Arlo, Audrey, and Jackie

Text © 1999 by Perfection Learning® Corporation.
All rights reserved. No part of this book may be used or reproduced in
any manner whatsoever without written permission from the publisher.
Printed in the United States of America. For information, contact
Perfection Learning® Corporation
Phone: 1-800-831-4190
Fax: 1-712-644-2392
1000 North Second Avenue, P.O. Box 500
Logan, Iowa 51546-1099.
Paperback ISBN 0-7891-2377-0
CoverCraft© ISBN 0-7807-7742-5
7 8 9 10 PP 09 08 07 06 05 04

Contents

1

Leaving Again

It didn't take me long to gather my things. Mrs. Bane, the caseworker from Multnomah County Children's Services, had come to pick me up. And I'd only been at this foster home for two weeks!

I stuffed what I had into a sack. Two pairs of jeans and three shirts. A coat with a broken zipper that was worn out at the elbows. Socks, underwear, and a ratty, old sweater.

That sweater had been my Christmas present at the shelter last year. Some half-blind old senior citizen had knitted it. Then she donated it to the shelter. Bless her old soul!

It was two shades of blue. But it was only supposed to be one. You could see right across the back where she'd run out of the first shade and started with another. One sleeve was about a foot longer than the other. The back hit me down around my knees. And the front was even with my belly button. The neck was so small that when I buttoned the top button my eyes bulged out and I couldn't breathe.

It was one crummy sweater. And I said so in front of the people who worked at the shelter. So I got a whopper of a lecture. Lectures were a big thing at the shelter.

I had some personal junk like my toothbrush, a comb, and a fingernail file. The shelter had given them to me. The people at the shelter always made sure we took them to a new foster home. It was very important to be clean and well-groomed. Cleanliness was next to godliness and all that stuff.

Mrs. Bane was in the kitchen drinking coffee with Mrs. Seits. So I went outside and sat on the front steps. I left the door open a little. I was a whiz at eavesdropping.

In between the traffic noises I could hear parts of what Mrs. Seits said.

"His attitude . . . smart-mouthed . . . recalcitrant . . . couldn't leave anything of value out in sight . . . even took money out of my purse! And the way he treated poor Loran! After all, Loran's only ten and Patrick is twelve. And he is—well, you know—worldly."

Worldly?! I could have thrown up.

When I get mad I spit. And right then I spit and spit and spit! Sometimes I get so mad I almost dehydrate.

Boy, was Mrs. Seits leaving a lot out! Well, if *recalcitrant* means bad, she was right about that. I'm recalcitrant because I hate foster parents.

Foster parents are all a bunch of goody-goodies. Or they're in it for the money. Most of them can't stand foster kids any more than I can stand them.

And sure, I snitched money out of Mrs. Seits's purse. But no more money than her precious little lard-rumped son, Loran.

And maybe I *was* smart-mouthed, but I wasn't any more smart-mouthed than she was. She called me things like "welfare brat" and "snot-nosed liar." And *she* didn't get smacked across the mouth for it like I did.

Of course, I was pretty used to being smacked around. I'd been smacked around a lot in my life. Even before I started getting placed in foster homes. Way back when I was just a little runt still wetting my pants. In fact, that's one of the things I remember getting smacked around for—wetting my pants.

I was living with my mother then. And some weirdo named Rick something. He was a long-haired doper. I was just a little kid then. And I was scared to death of him.

I never knew *who* my father was or *where* he was. The first time I asked my mother, she said that he'd died before I was born. She must have forgotten telling me that, though. Because the next time I asked her, she said she didn't know. It was no big deal anyway. I didn't need a father. I didn't need *anybody*.

I think this Rick guy got my mother hooked on dope. Not the hard stuff—that came later.

After Rick got busted, a guy named Al moved in. After that, a couple of other guys whose names I forgot. Al wasn't too bad. Even if he was on the hard stuff. He treated me okay. Except for one time.

Al and some of his friends got me drunk on some wine. Man, was I sick! They all laughed their heads off when I staggered around and threw up all over myself. I don't remember my mother laughing. But she didn't make them stop.

But back to Rick. I couldn't help wetting myself. Whenever I cried or got scared, it just ran down my legs. There wasn't a thing I could do about it.

One time a couple of bigger kids that lived in the project where we lived had a rope. They were trying to tie me up. I got loose and ran home, screaming bloody murder and wetting my pants.

I remember that Mom told Rick how I couldn't help it.

Rick just yelled, "By God, he'll help it or else!"

Rick pulled my wet pants down. Then he smacked me on my bare bottom again and again with the flat of his hand. I screamed so hard I couldn't catch my breath. I guess I must have passed out.

The next thing I knew, I woke up in my bed in the middle of the night. Mom and Rick had gone out. I was all alone. I didn't like waking up in the middle of the night and finding out I was all alone. It was scary.

I couldn't sit down for about a week. Man, I hated that Rick!

Every once in a while, Mrs. Bane got a word in. She used a lot of psychology talk like "his traumatic experiences" and "taking out his hostilities" and "adjusting to circumstances."

Good old Mrs. Bane! She was always on my side. Well, almost always. And she wasn't really *old*. As a matter of fact, she was pretty young.

Mrs. Seits didn't seem to be falling for any of it.

"It's not that I don't feel for Patrick," Mrs. Seits said. "I know his life hasn't exactly been a bed of roses. And having a mother like that. Well, what can you expect?"

I put my hands over my ears and pushed until it hurt. Stop it! Stop it! I wanted to scream. She's *my* mother! You have no right to talk about her! She's my mother! She's mine! And I—I hate her!

I felt a lump sticking in my throat. I stood up so I could swallow it better. I got it down just as Mrs. Seits and Mrs. Bane walked out.

Mrs. Seits had the gooiest smile on her face. She patted me on the head.

"I'm really sorry, Patrick, that things didn't work out," Mrs. Seits said. "Mr. Seits and I will miss you."

Mr. Seits! What a laugh! Mr. Seits wasn't allowed to *think* without her permission.

My right hand was working into a fist. I pushed it into my pocket. If I hadn't, I might have smashed it right into that big, fat stomach of hers. It was a good thing Loran was in school. I don't think I could have resisted the urge to clobber him good before I left.

Mrs. Bane didn't say a word until we got into the car. Then she let me have it. She had a way of telling you off without even getting mad. But when she got through, you knew you'd been told off. I couldn't count the times I'd "disappointed" her.

I'd known Mrs. Bane since I was six. That's when my mother OD'd for the third time and flipped out. So the doctors sent her to that place. She wanted to kill herself. But the doctors didn't want her to. They had to watch my mother all the time to make sure she didn't do it. I didn't know why they cared, but they did.

The doctors released her once on a kind of trial thing. I was eight years old. It was neat having a real home again. I'd already been in four foster homes, besides all the time I had spent at the shelter.

My mother had been home for about a month. One day, I ran home from school all excited because I'd gotten the lead in the Christmas play. I could hardly wait to tell her. I came tearing around the corner of our apartment building.

An ambulance was parked at the curb. Two men were carrying out a stretcher. My mother was on it. The strong smell of gas was coming from the building. I never got to be in that Christmas play. I spent Christmas at the shelter.

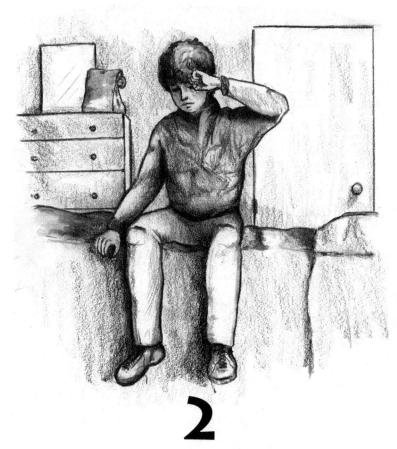

2
Temporary Homes

Mrs. Bane didn't say anything as we drove about ten blocks in the city traffic. Then she finally gave the big sigh she always started with.

"Well, Patrick Engstrom," Mrs. Bane said. "Here we go again."

I didn't say anything. But I glanced at her out of the corner of my eye.

You couldn't tell much by Mrs. Bane's face unless you knew her as well as I did. And I knew her well enough to tell that she was disappointed in me—a lot.

"Do you have any idea how many times this makes, Pat?" Mrs. Bane asked.

I didn't answer. But I *did* know. It made sixteen times.

I couldn't remember too much about the first foster home. Except that I was scared and cried a lot. The foster parents spanked me for crying, but it didn't work. They finally just sent me back to the shelter.

The second, third, and fourth were all about the same. One was a religious couple. They'd never had any kids of their own. And they kept telling me they were going to adopt me as soon as God sent them a sign. They spanked me or sent me to my room without dinner lots of times. They said it was because God told them to. They said the devil had ahold of me. And they were doing the Christian thing by whipping him out of me. It was a constant battle between them and the devil.

Then one day, the foster parents were in the process of "making Satan let go." And Mrs. Bane happened to drop by. Well, that ended that.

One foster woman had a guy who used to come every few days while her husband was at work. She made me and another foster kid she was keeping stay outside while he was there. The guy was her boyfriend, but I didn't know it. I figured that out after I got older.

There was one family that was okay. The McBrides. They were kind of middle-aged. Mr. McBride took me fishing and taught me to play checkers. He even let me help him work on his car. Mrs. McBride baked bread and cakes and pies. She made me a red plaid shirt. I really liked that shirt.

Then just like that—I'd been there about three months—she got really sick and died. I couldn't stay with just Mr. McBride, even if he wanted me.

That's when I decided I wouldn't get too worked up about finding a permanent home. There just weren't too many people around like the McBrides.

Mrs. Bane stopped for a red light. She looked me right in the face.

"I'm disappointed in you, Pat," Mrs. Bane said. "You know, you blew it again."

"Maybe *she* blew it!" I snapped. "Mrs. Seits and that pig-faced kid of hers. Besides, I'd just as soon stay at the shelter as I would any old foster home."

Mrs. Bane gave that big sigh again.

"You see, Pat," she began. "There's a chance you may not be staying at either."

I jerked around in the seat and faced her. I knew what she was going to say. Then I made myself calm down and lean back on the seat.

"What's that mean?" I asked, real cool.

"The shelter is only a temporary home," Mrs. Bane explained. "Until a proper foster home can be found." She reached over and touched my arm. "When a youngster doesn't adjust to foster homes—"

I butted in before Mrs. Bane could finish. "They get sent to Woodlawn," I said. "So?"

"Is that what you want, Pat?" Mrs. Bane asked. "I find that hard to believe."

"It makes no difference to me where I go," I lied, nearly choking. "One place is as good as another."

I was getting goose pimples just thinking about getting sent to Woodlawn. I'd almost gone there once. For shoplifting and running away so many times. But right at the last minute, the judge changed his mind. He sent me to another foster home. That's when I ended up with the McBrides.

Woodlawn is called a home for boys. But it's nothing but a prison for guys who aren't old enough to be sent to the state pen. Some of the kids at the shelter had been in Woodlawn. So I'd heard all about it. I'd take the worst foster home any day. But I'd die before I'd let Mrs. Bane or anyone else know.

After spending two weeks with that Seits bunch, the old shelter looked pretty good. I knew some of the kids at the shelter. Kids who had been in and out of foster homes the same as me.

Randy Carver was back there again. He was waiting for his mother to get paroled from the women's state pen. It was her second time up for forgery. But they were letting her out so she could take care of her kids. Randy had three little sisters who were living with relatives. And the relatives were getting tired of taking care of them.

Bill Swartz was there again. He had more trouble with foster homes than I did. He was only going to be there a little while. Arrangements were being made to send him to a place for kids with special problems. Bill was a little retarded.

Nick Cheevers came back the day before I did. He'd been in Woodlawn again. It was his second time. He was all worked up about a foster home he was going to in about a week. The foster dad was a teacher and basketball coach. Nick was crazy about basketball. All he ever dreamed of was the NBA. He was a couple of years older than me and almost six feet tall.

"This may be my big chance, Pat," Nick said to me that first day back at the shelter. "I'm good. I know I am."

I encouraged him the best I could. "You'll make it, Nick," I said. "In a few years, you'll be playing with the Blazers."

Nick shrugged his shoulders. "I don't know," he said. "Seems like I was born for trouble." He shook his head. "But no, I'm not blowing a chance like this. No way!"

Nick and I had been best friends for a long time. Nick was the one I'd run off with the time I almost got sent to Woodlawn. Nick *did* get sent there. I figured it was because he was older. He never resented me because I got off. He was that kind of guy.

It had been really neat when we ran away together. Even if we did end up in a real mess when we got caught. We'd shoplifted a package of cookies and some cans of baked beans. We'd never even made it out of the city limits. But we were able to hide out for three days. Then we were hauled back to the shelter.

Hiding out was a blast! One night we hid in a closet in a department store just before closing time. And we spent the night there. We slept in a tent that was set up in the sporting goods department. We were still asleep the next morning when the store opened. But no one discovered us. When the store got crowded, we just crawled out.

I wondered if I'd ever see Nick again. I hoped he would make it at his new foster home. It sure would be something if he turned out to be a pro basketball player. Especially after all he'd been through.

"Hey, that's my good buddy, Nick Cheevers," I'd say to everyone. "I knew him when we were kids. We ran away together once."

It was sad the day Nick left for his new foster home. We punched each other on the arm and said, "See ya around."

After I'd been at the shelter for several months, I started getting worried. Maybe they weren't trying to find any more foster homes for me. Maybe I really did blow it this time. They were probably planning to send me to Woodlawn. Nick had said it was really crowded the last time he was in. As soon as there was an opening, they'd be sending me, I thought.

I wondered if they'd let my mother know. But it wouldn't make any difference to her. She wouldn't care.

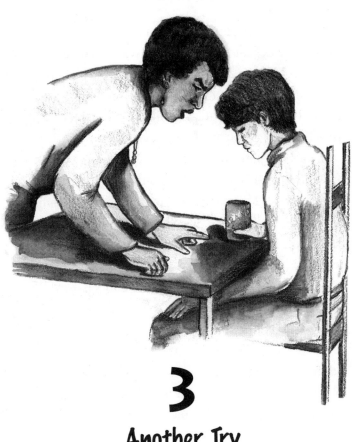

3

Another Try

I hated school. I'd hated it right from the very first day. That's when most kids were all excited about going to school.

My mother had already been sent to that place. I was in my first foster home. They were the people who sent me back for crying so much.

The first foster parents didn't take me to school the first day. They just told me which way to go and sent me alone. I had to cross a really busy street. There were traffic lights. But I'd never crossed a busy street before. I was scared stiff. The light changed three times before I got up enough nerve to cross.

I heard the bell ringing when I was about a block from the school. There weren't any kids on the playground. I'd been warned about getting in trouble if I was late. So I broke into a run. When I did reach the school, I was breathing hard. And it was all I could do to open the heavy doors.

I finally found my classroom. When I sat down in the seat, my teacher pointed at me. That's when I realized my pants were soaking wet.

When I was at the shelter, I'd go to school there. We had three or four grades in one room. Depending on how many kids there were at the shelter at the time.

I was supposed to be in the seventh grade. But I had moved around so much I was a year behind. I was just barely making it in the sixth. Once, I'd counted how many schools I'd gone to. Not counting the school at the shelter, I'd gone to 12 schools. And I had done lousy in every one of them. I even got held back in the second grade.

The reason I was just *one* year behind was that one of my fourth-grade teachers felt sorry for me. I flunked every subject. But she passed me anyway. She figured my being that far behind would only add to my "problems."

So I struggled along, wondering what the heck all that stuff in books was good for. I couldn't read a whole sentence without making at least three mistakes. Even if they were short sentences. Words threw me for a loop.

The school at the shelter was always needing teachers. And they almost always had more kids than they were supposed to.

This time I had a teacher I'd never seen before. She looked like she should be riding a broom with a black cat behind her. Even her name fit her—Elvira Skogg.

Right away, I didn't like her. She seemed to take a real dislike to me too. I decided it was because I was dumb. And that made her look bad.

When it was my turn to read, she'd get this really disgusted look on her face. It was like I was something that should be in a garbage can. She'd stand over me shaking her head real slow. And I'd stumble over the words. She wouldn't even help me.

Just knowing that she was looking at me like that made it harder for me to read. I started stuttering. Not just when I was reading, but a lot of other times too. Like when I got nervous.

Some of the kids started teasing me about it. Especially one ape-faced bully named Marvin Repler.

One day at dinner, Marvin started giving me a bad time.

"Hey, P-P-P-Pat. P-p-p-pass the b-b-b-butter," Marvin teased. He was grinning like an ape.

All the guys at our table busted out laughing.

Usually, I have a lot more sense than to tackle a guy twice my size. But with all that laughter roaring in my ears, I got so mad I lost my senses.

I dived across the table, sliding through mashed potatoes and gravy and raspberry Jell-O. Marvin's chair toppled over. He landed on his back with me on his chest.

I just happened to have a chicken drumstick in my hand. When it came to me what a dumb thing I'd done, I rammed that drumstick down Marvin's throat. I figured if I wanted to keep from getting killed when he got up, I'd have to kill him first. And I darn near did.

Someone pulled me off Marvin. But not before I gave the drumstick an extra hard shove. Old Marvin gagged and slobbered. His eyes bulged out. And all of a sudden, he gave a huge cough. That drumstick shot three feet straight up in the air.

Boy, was I in trouble! Trouble wasn't anything new to me. But that didn't mean I liked it. And I liked it a whole lot less when the trouble was because of some creep like Marvin Repler.

The people at the shelter were setting up a hearing date for the following week. The hearing was to decide what my punishment should be for "viciously attacking another person."

Then Miss Skogg, the old witch teacher, said I couldn't do sixth-grade work. She wanted to put me back in fifth.

On top of everything else, I was terrified of running into Marvin. I knew he'd kill me for sure. But guess what? I ran into him the very next day. And he acted like I didn't even exist. His eyes were still a little bulgy.

Only one good thing came out of the fight in the cafeteria. Just like that, I stopped stuttering. I never stuttered again.

The day before the hearing date, I decided to split. What did I have to lose? If I got caught, I'd get sent to Woodlawn. When they had the hearing and saw all my faults, the verdict would be Woodlawn anyway.

After all, I'd been back at the shelter for months. They probably weren't even trying to place me again. I was too dumb and unwilling to adjust to foster homes. I knew what they were thinking.

I kept thinking how neat it would be if Nick could go with me. Just like last time. Only this time I planned on going south. All the way to California. I figured once I got there, they'd never find me.

I was in old lady Skogg's classroom struggling through a sentence in my reader. The old witch was glaring at me. Then the door opened, and in walked Wonder Woman. Well, actually, it was Mrs. Bane. But she could have been Wonder Woman at that moment.

Before she finished talking to Miss Skogg, she motioned me out in the hall. But I was already putting away my books and stuff and heading toward her. I was having a hard time playing it cool. Like it was no big deal, her showing up after all that time. I had decided she'd given up on me like everyone else.

When we got out in the hall, Mrs. Bane looked down at me.

"Well, Pat," Mrs. Bane said. "How's it going?"

"It's okay," I answered, shrugging.

"Oh, really?" she asked. "That's not the way I hear it. Sounds like anything but okay to me."

I quietly sucked in my breath. Oh-oh! She knew all about the mess I was in. I supposed she had just dropped by to tell me good-bye and good luck and all that rot before I got sent up. I had to admit that Mrs. Bane had done just about everything anyone *could* do for me.

But heck, it wasn't my fault I didn't have a regular home. It wasn't my fault I didn't like living with

24

strangers. It wasn't my fault that *she* was locked up in a booby-hatch. Just because she wanted to kill herself and didn't want to take care of me. Oh well, I thought. By this time tomorrow, I'll be long gone.

I was glad Mrs. Bane dropped by anyway. Even under the circumstances, it was neat to see her.

"Anything you want to talk about?" she asked.

"Nothing to talk about," I answered. "A guy just hassled me once too often, and I let him have it. What's wrong with that?"

They were sure making a big deal out of it. I felt good knowing I had more than held my own with that big ape.

"Are you going to be at the hearing tomorrow?" I asked. I wondered if that was why she showed up after so long.

Mrs. Bane didn't say anything. She took me by the arm, and we walked down the hall. She took me to a break room.

Mrs. Bane took two cans of pop out of the refrigerator. She handed one to me and told me to sit down. She took a swallow of her pop.

"Yes, I'm going to be at the hearing," she said. "If there is a hearing."

I stared at her. "What do you mean *if?*" I asked. "Why *wouldn't* there be a hearing?"

What was she talking about, anyway? Had they already decided? She was making me nervous, sitting there like that and not answering.

"Is there going to be a hearing or not?" I yelled at her.

She smiled. "You haven't changed a bit, have you, Pat?"

"You could answer me," I said, but not as loud.

"There may not be a hearing," said Mrs. Bane. "I guess you might say it's up to you."

"Huh?" was all I could think of to say.

"I know you don't like foster homes," she said. "But if you're willing to give it one more try . . ."

"Okay, okay," I said—a lot faster than I meant to. "I'll go along with whatever you have in mind. If it'll make you happy."

I shouldn't have added that. For the first time since I'd known Mrs. Bane, she came unglued. She was more than "disappointed" in me. She was mad!

"Now just a cotton-pickin' minute, young man!" she said sternly. I thought she might even take a swing at me. "I'll have you know, I have worked my tail off for you! If it had been up to anyone else, you would have been in Woodlawn a long time ago. Now I've found a home for you with some very nice people. The choice is up to you."

Before I could draw in my breath to say a word, she continued. "But I want this understood. If you blow it this time, you are on your own. Understood?"

I nodded.

"Fine," she said. "I'll be here at 8:00 in the morning. Make sure you're ready."

"How come so early?" I asked.

"Because it's a long drive," Mrs. Bane said. "It'll take about two hours to get there."

She led me through the door and back down the hall to the classroom. I turned around to ask, "Where is this place?"

But she was gone.

4

What's the Catch?

I had a hard time falling asleep that night. There were so many things I was wondering about.

Who were these people that Mrs. Bane had dug up? She said they were very nice. Well, how did she know that? A lot of foster parents were very nice at the beginning. That didn't mean a thing.

And just because they were very nice to Mrs. Bane didn't mean they would be nice to me. I was an expert on foster parents. I knew how tricky they could be.

I wondered if they had other kids. If they did, I hoped they weren't like Loran Seits and some of the others I'd known. I wouldn't mind other kids if they didn't try to boss me around and get me in trouble. A kid my age would be okay, *if* he wasn't a creep.

Which kind were these people going to turn out to be? The religious goody-goodies? Or the ones who were in it for the money? They didn't pay a lot to foster parents. But if they worked it right, they could come out on top.

Before I knew it, it was 8:00. I'd gulped down breakfast and said good-bye to the few friends I had. I wished I could say good-bye to Nick.

Mrs. Bane was right on time, like I knew she'd be. I followed her out to her car. It was parked at the curb. I was careful not to look back. The shelter wasn't anything I wanted to remember. Man, I hoped I'd never have to see it again.

I'd promised Mrs. Bane I'd go along with the deal. But deep down inside, I knew I wanted no part of foster homes. They were all alike. Oh, I knew of some kids who had made out all right. Some even ended up getting adopted. But me—I wasn't born that lucky.

If this place turned out like the others, I'd split so fast they wouldn't know what had happened. But I wouldn't blame Mrs. Bane. Not after all she'd tried to do for me. I might blame a lot of other people, mostly *her*—but I wouldn't blame Mrs. Bane.

After a while I realized that we weren't even in town anymore. Nothing looked familiar to me. I knew Portland like the back of my hand. I'd lived in almost every part of it at one time or another.

I looked around, puzzled. We were on the freeway. "Hey," I said. "Where are we? And where are we going?"

"Just outside Lebanon," Mrs. Bane answered.

"Lebanon!" I exclaimed. "That's another country! It's across the ocean!"

Man, they were *really* getting rid of me!

Mrs. Bane started laughing so hard I thought she was going to run off the road.

"What's so funny?" I yelled.

"Patrick," Mrs. Bane was still chuckling. "For a native Oregonian, you don't know much about Oregon."

"You mean there's a place called Lebanon in Oregon?" I asked.

"Yes," said Mrs. Bane. "I should know. I was born and raised there."

"Well, where is it?" I wanted to know.

30

"It's in the Willamette Valley on the Santiam River," replied Mrs. Bane. "In a very beautiful location."

"How big is it?" I wondered.

"Well, not big at all," said Mrs. Bane.

"In other words," I concluded, "it's a hick town."

"By your standards, maybe," laughed Mrs. Bane.

"I don't like hick towns," I stated.

"Oh, really," she said smugly. "When was the last time you lived in one? And exactly what is a hick town?"

"Well—uh—they probably got dumb schools." I wished I hadn't said that.

"No doubt." Sometimes Mrs. Bane could be so maddening, like right then.

"How about these people?" I asked.

"Mitch and Lynn Kelly are two of the nicest people I know. I went to school with Lynn," she said. "They've only been married a couple of years. Mitch's father died about a year ago, and his mother went to Idaho to live with a daughter. Mitch and Lynn moved to the old home place. Lynn is expecting."

"Expecting!" I practically screamed.

"That's right," she said. "Expecting. In other words, pregnant."

I knew what it meant, for Pete's sake. It was just that I'd never been around anyone who was expecting. I knew that pregnant women got fat and threw up a lot. It sounded gross.

"Oh, great," I moaned. "So that's the catch."

Mrs. Bane wrinkled up her forehead and looked at me. "Catch?"

"The reason they want a foster kid," I said. "To take care of the baby. Well, if they think I'm going to do it, they're nuts. I'm not going to take care of any bawling brat."

"Are you through?" Mrs. Bane was "disappointed" in me again.

I said, "Yeah, I'm through—for now."

"If they wanted someone to take care of a baby," said Mrs. Bane, "I'm sure they could have found someone with—well, a little better disposition."

"What's that mean?"

"I can tell you this," she said. "I wouldn't want you to take care of any baby of mine. If it didn't do things to suit you, you'd probably—probably take it to the dog pound."

For some reason that struck me funny. Taking a baby to the dog pound. I started giggling. Mrs. Bane must have thought it sounded funny too, because she started giggling.

The next thing I knew Mrs. Bane was saying, "This is Lebanon, Pat."

I sat up straight and started looking around. We were on Main Street. There was a department store, a couple of banks, three restaurants, a grocery store, a service station, some offices, and a theater.

"This is it?" I asked, craning my neck. I was trying to see down the side streets.

"Just about," she said.

She turned off Main Street. We went a few blocks, crossed a bridge, and that was the end of town.

Mrs. Bane was right about one thing. The town was pretty. We passed a field full of sheep with some lambs. Mrs. Bane said most of the lambs would be born a little later. I didn't say it out loud, but I thought they were about the cutest things I'd ever seen. I wished I could hold one.

After a while Mrs. Bane turned off the paved road and drove down a gravel road. We stopped in front of a white house that was trimmed in green.

While Mrs. Bane was giving me instructions— "Please, Patrick, use your manners. Try to be friendly"—I looked things over. The house was old but nice. There were lots of trees and shrubs. There were some buildings behind the house. There was a white picket fence across the front of the yard. It was a pretty neat setup.

There was something that was still puzzling me. "How come I'm going to a foster home so far away from Portland? I thought I was supposed to stay in Multnomah County."

"I had to pull plenty of strings," she answered. "I thought maybe a change might—might do you some good. I'm hoping it will." She looked right at me and said, "You know I won't be your caseworker anymore, Pat. But I'd like to keep in touch. I'll miss you."

I didn't tell her, but I'd miss her too.

"Another thing," I said. "How come someone who is young and hasn't been married very long and is going to have a baby is taking in a foster kid? They need the dough?"

Mrs. Bane smiled. "I'm sure they don't. Mitch has a very good job. He's a foreman at the plywood mill." She touched my arm. "There's a very simple reason, even though you may have a little trouble believing it. Mitch and Lynn are nice people who happen to like kids."

"But they're going to have a kid of their own," I argued. "Why would they want me?"

She grinned—really grinned. "Maybe they've heard what a sweet boy you are."

Before I could answer, the door of the house opened, and Lynn came out. Even though she was as pregnant as she could be, she was some chick. She was young, like Mrs. Bane. Most foster mothers were old.

When Mrs. Bane and I got to the porch—of all things—Lynn threw her arms around me and hugged the heck out of me. Talk about embarrassing!

She said, "I'm so glad you're finally here." She planted a big, fat kiss right on my cheek.

Mrs. McBride was the only foster mother that ever kissed me. And then only when I was leaving for school or something. They were just little pecks too.

Lynn dragged me by the hand and said, "I have chocolate chip cookies that just came out of the oven. And there's icy cold milk to go with them."

Man, what a stack of cookies there was on the kitchen table. I'd never seen that many cookies all at once. I ate six with my first glass of milk. And five with my second.

All Lynn said was, "Glad you like them. They're Mitch's favorite."

I remembered what Mrs. Bane had said about my manners. "They're the best I ever tasted. Thank you."

I caught Mrs. Bane's pleased look.

Lynn said, "Let me show you where you'll be bunking."

I picked up my bag and followed her down a long hall. Wow! What a room it was! Not fancy or anything, but nice. And big. The walls were blue. I was sure they had just been painted. For me? One wall had built-in cupboards and shelves from the floor to the ceiling.

Lynn said it was to store all my belongings. I thought if I lived to be a hundred, I'd never own enough stuff to fill up all those shelves. There was a big picture window that looked out across a field. In the background were mountains with snow on them.

It was the neatest room any kid could have.

Everything about the Kellys' place was nice. The house had big cozy rooms. There was an old-fashioned stove in the kitchen that burned wood. Lynn said Mitch's father and mother had bought it when they first moved into the house. There was an electric stove too. The fireplace in the living room was made from huge stones. Lynn told me Mitch's grandfather had made it when he built the house years and years ago.

"There were over a hundred acres then, but only five acres are left," Lynn said. "We don't really farm, but we have fruit and berries. And we grow a big garden in the summer. You might like to join 4-H. If you do, there's plenty of room to raise an animal for a project."

I said I'd think about it. I didn't know much about 4-H, but raising an animal sounded pretty cool. I thought about the lambs I'd seen on the way.

Lynn said when Mitch got home, he'd show me around outside. I was dying to walk through the woods at the back of the property. But I wouldn't say so. I wasn't ready to open up. I hadn't made up my mind about things. How could there not be a catch?

Mrs. Bane didn't get mushy when she said good-bye. She asked me to write and let her know how things were going.

How *would* things be going? I wondered. Things were never too bad at first. It took a while before people showed themselves the way they really were.

I said maybe I'd write to her.

I didn't care what Mrs. Bane had said. There had to be a catch. There just had to be.

I stayed inside the house when Mrs. Bane left. I didn't want to watch her drive off down the road. I felt like there was something stuck in the pit of my stomach.

5

Traps

It's a real funny feeling—the first few days in a new foster home. There you are, face to face with complete strangers. You feel like you're on a slide, and they're looking at you through a microscope.

The bad thing is they know all about you. About your past and your problems and your family and everything. And you don't know a thing about them. Not at first anyway. But you learn in a big hurry.

The nights are the worst. It's hard to fall asleep in a strange bed in a strange house. So you lie awake and think. And that's the worst part of all—the thinking.

I felt uncomfortable after Mrs. Bane left. Being alone with someone I didn't know was bad enough. But Lynn being so pregnant made me even more nervous. I couldn't seem to keep from staring at her stomach—no matter how hard I tried. I hoped she didn't notice. I didn't want her to think I was a dirty-minded kid.

I didn't feel uncomfortable for very long. Lynn didn't let me.

"Do you like music, Pat?" Lynn asked me.

She was shuffling toward the stereo before I could answer. I was expecting some of that stuff that lots of grown-ups go for. But was I ever wrong. Not only was it my kind of music, it was loud.

"I'll fix us a bite for lunch," Lynn yelled over the music. "I hope you like hot dogs."

I *love* hot dogs. I ate two with a bowl of tomato soup and more cookies.

After lunch, we put my few things away in my room. Then Lynn taught me a real fun card game. We played cards, listened to music, and talked the rest of the afternoon.

Then Mitch came home. The way he acted, you'd think I'd been there every day when he came home from work. It was like I was someone he'd known a long time. And it was the strangest thing, but I almost felt that way about him too.

"There's not much daylight left, Pat," Mitch said, washing his hands in the kitchen sink. "But I'll take you out and show you around if you want."

Boy, were those woods neat! I had a thing about trees. I really liked them. I wondered what they felt like waving their tops around way up there. Looking down on everything.

"Nice, huh?"

I must have jumped a foot when Mitch said that. I thought for a minute I'd said that dumb thing out loud—about the trees.

"We've never done a thing to this little patch of woods," Mitch said. "My grandfather and my father farmed all around it. Then Dad got sick. He and Mom sold most of the land. All but five acres."

Mitch looked up at the treetops and smiled. He had a great smile. It crinkled up his whole face. He wasn't a bad-looking guy. He was really tall with broad shoulders. For a big man, he had the softest voice I'd ever heard.

He smiled at those trees for quite a while. "These are God's trees," he said after a while. "That's why we've never touched them. They're just the way God meant for them to grow."

Oh, brother! I thought. Is that the catch? Are they a pair of religious nuts? The kind that like to take in foster kids and save their souls? I'd seen a lot of them. But it didn't seem like Mitch was one of them. Or Lynn either.

A few minutes later, I knew for sure Mitch wasn't a religious nut.

Out of the clear blue sky, Mitch bent over and jerked something up from the ground. He started beating it against a fallen log. He was using some language that no religious nut ever used. I didn't know what it was all about. But I knew he was one mad guy.

The thing Mitch was banging against the log was metal. It had a chain on it. As near as I could tell, it had little points on it—kind of like a saw.

Mitch sat down on the log, holding that thing in one hand. He was breathing hard. The only part of the outburst that I had understood was something about "those lousy Crumps."

I wondered what the heck a "crump" was. I asked Mitch.

"Our so-called neighbors," Mitch panted. "Hank and Rose Crump. And their oversized oaf of a kid, Otis."

"What's that thing?" I asked. I pointed at whatever was still hanging from his right hand.

"This is called a leg-hold trap," Mitch said.

"What's it for?" I asked.

"That's a good question, Pat," he said.

Mitch was still really mad. He told me about trapping. How animals were attracted by the bait. And how those steel jaws snapped down on an animal's leg. Then I was mad too!

"Otis gets his kicks out of trapping," Mitch said. "All the Crump boys did. The other three boys have left home. Otis is the only one left."

Mitch took a deep breath and went on. "Those boys were never particular about whose land they set their traps on. Or what they caught in them. We've had to have two cats put to sleep because they got caught in traps."

"Why would anyone want to catch animals in traps?" I asked.

"Mostly for their furs," replied Mitch. "And sheep ranchers set traps for coyotes that kill their sheep."

"Can't they keep them out some other way?" I asked.

"Probably," said Mitch. "But trapping is easier and cheaper."

Mitch showed me how a trap was set. The chain was fastened to something solid and covered with dirt.

"The animal comes to the trap for the bait and steps on the trigger," Mitch explained. "Then the spring releases. The jaws snap around the animal's leg with great force. Some traps have teeth like this one. The teeth make it much more painful for the animal."

I felt like I was going to be sick. I turned my head so Mitch couldn't see my face. But then he started telling me how I should spring any trap I ever found set on the property. I had to turn around and watch how it was done.

Before we got back to the house, Mitch had said, "We won't say anything to Lynn about the trap until after dinner."

It was nearly dark when we got back to the house. Mitch dropped the trap in the trash can.

When I saw the meal that Lynn had fixed, I felt a little better. Lynn sure could cook. And Mitch sure could eat.

I was surprised that I felt so relaxed with Lynn and Mitch. I'd only known them for a few hours. I couldn't help thinking that Mrs. Bane had hit the nail on the head this time.

But I hadn't been there very long. If there was ever an expert on foster parents, it was me. And these two just didn't fit the pattern. But for now, I had to admit that this was the best foster home I'd ever been in.

Lynn finished the dishes. And Mitch built a fire in the fireplace. Lynn asked me to go into the utility room and bring her the dishes that were on the floor. Until then, I didn't even know they had pets.

Lynn stood on the back porch and called for a long time. Finally, a big, fat, black and white cat came in.

"This is Toby," Lynn said.

Lynn set a bowl of canned food in front of the cat. Toby gulped it down like he was starved. But as fat as he was, I didn't think he'd missed many meals in his life.

I bent down to pet Toby, but he moved away and meowed.

"Toby's a one-woman cat," Lynn said. "He barely tolerates Mitch. Give him time. He'll get used to you."

Lynn filled the other bowl with dog food. Then she banged on the bowl with a spoon and yelled bloody murder. "Here, Shorty! Here, Shorty! Come and get it, boy!" She just about broke my eardrums!

After a while, a brown, bow-legged, floppy-eared dog came waddling into the kitchen from the living room. He sniffed at my shoes a couple of times and then waddled over to his bowl. The entire time he was eating, he snorted.

"Poor old Shorty is almost deaf," Lynn said. "And his eyesight is poor. He's 14 years old. We inherited him along with the place."

When he finished eating, Shorty sniffed my shoes some more.

"He likes to have his back scratched," said Lynn.

Did he ever! The harder I scratched, the more he grunted.

I liked the idea of living someplace with pets. The only place I could remember that had pets was the McBrides'. They had canaries and parakeets. Birds were nice, but I thought I would like dogs and cats better.

When I stopped scratching Shorty, he waddled back into the living room. He crawled into a low basket in the corner. I discovered later that that was where he spent most of his life. He only woke up long enough to eat and go outside to do his thing. Once in a while, he'd come to one of us and snort until we scratched him.

We didn't do much that first evening but talk. I saw a TV in the corner, but Lynn and Mitch didn't turn it on. Mitch said we were spending the evening getting to know one another. They didn't ask me a lot of questions—like about any of the trouble I'd been in. Or the other foster homes. Or about my mother.

Some of the foster parents, like old lady Seits, just about pumped me to death. She kept asking about things that I figured were none of her darn business.

Mrs. Seits kept asking me about my father. At first, I tried to tell her I didn't know anything about him. And that I'd never seen him. One day, she said, "Are you sure you don't know anything at all about him, Patrick?"

I couldn't resist it. I said, "Well—all I remember is he was big and ugly. And he had a glass eye that he

45

used to take out and let me play with. Until one day when I swallowed it."

She called me a little liar and smacked me across the mouth. But it was worth it. She never asked me about my father again.

Lynn and Mitch didn't ask me any of those kinds of things. They just wanted to know my birthday, my favorite foods, colors, songs, television programs. You know—that kind of stuff.

Then they asked me my favorite subject in school. I said none of them, and they just laughed. Mitch said maybe I needed a little tutoring and that Lynn was good at tutoring. Then an awful thought crossed my mind. When they found out how dumb I was, they might send me back.

Mitch finally told Lynn about finding the trap. Man, did she ever hit the ceiling! She said the same things about the Crumps that Mitch had. I thought those Crumps must be a really bad bunch. I was dying to meet Otis. Lynn said he was in grade school even though he was old enough to be in high school.

"He'd better never let me catch him setting traps on our place," Lynn said. "He'll wish he had never been born."

That first day went smooth. But, I reminded myself, it was only the first day. This might just be the bait. Maybe Otis wasn't the only one who had set a trap.

You're nuts, I told myself.

Well, the first day ended great. Except—of all things—I had a terrible nightmare.

I dreamed about the time they took my mother away. After she turned on the gas. She was on a stretcher, and men were putting her in an ambulance. I was screaming bloody murder. "No! No! Don't take her away! Don't take her away!" I tried to get to her, but I was caught in a giant trap. It was cutting into my ankle. And the gas fumes coming from the apartment building were choking me.

I must have screamed out loud because the lamp came on and there was Lynn. She sat on the edge of the bed and held me in her arms. She rocked me back and forth just like I was a little baby. She kept saying, "There now, there now. It's all right."

Lynn didn't even ask me what was the matter. She just kept rocking me until I fell asleep.

I had another dream later that night. I was a little kid—really little. I'd had a nightmare and woke up crying. Someone was holding me real close and rocking me back and forth saying, "There now, honey. It's all right."

It was my mother.

6

Fitting In

I got to Lynn and Mitch's place on Thursday. They said I didn't have to start school until Monday. If I'd had my way, it would have been a lot longer than that—like maybe forever.

Mrs. Bane had said that she wouldn't let me be put back into the fifth grade. That's what Miss Skogg wanted to do. But she said I had to give the sixth grade everything I had. Well, when it came to school, everything I had wouldn't make it in kindergarten.

On Friday, Lynn took me shopping for school clothes. When I saw the money that Lynn paid for everything, I couldn't believe it. Lynn and Mitch sure weren't in foster care for the money. Lynn had just spent more than the county would pay them in a month!

On top of everything else, Lynn bought me a basketball and a hoop.

"You and Mitch can spend tomorrow putting it up," Lynn said.

Then Lynn and I went out to lunch. That was the first time in my life I'd ever eaten in a real restaurant. We had shrimp, French fries, and salad. For dessert, we had apple pie and ice cream. It was great!

After Lynn and I had shopped and eaten lunch, we just walked around the town and looked it over. It only took about half an hour. It really wasn't a bad town. It just wasn't very big.

When we got home, Lynn made me model my new clothes. They were great clothes all right. Like nothing I'd ever owned in my life. She embarrassed the heck out of me the way she oohed and ahhed all over the place.

I showed Lynn my old blue sweater. The one with one arm a foot longer than the other. And the neck so small that it wouldn't even go around my wrist. She cracked up.

Then I had a brilliant idea. "I know just what this dumb old sweater is good for," I giggled.

I raised Shorty up just as far as I could—without his cooperation. Then I shoved the sweater underneath him. He opened his eyes and sniffed at it a couple of times. Then he went back to sleep.

Mitch made a big deal about my new clothes too. I didn't have to model them, but he looked them over and made some comments. "You'll be the best-dressed kid in school!" and "You'll sure have to fight off the girls!" He clapped me on the back.

I got really embarrassed again.

Saturday, Mitch and I put up the backboard and hoop. We shot baskets half the day. Mitch was good. It made me feel a little bit lonesome because it made me think of Nick Cheevers. I sure hoped things were going good for Nick. At least as good as they were for me—so far.

Monday morning came before I knew it. And before I was ready for it—that was for sure.

"I'll go with you the first day if you want me to, Pat," Lynn said.

Lynn couldn't guess how much I wanted her to. But I didn't want to be hassled by anyone about being brought to school like I was a baby. I sure didn't want to get in trouble right off the bat.

The school wasn't in town. It was a pretty small school district where everyone knew everyone else. It wasn't any big secret that Lynn and Mitch had taken in a foster kid.

Mitch left when I was just starting to eat breakfast. "See you tonight, Pat," he said. "Hang in there now."

Then Lynn started in. "Don't let anything bug you, Pat," she said. "Remember—everyone has been the new kid at one time or another."

What Lynn didn't know was that I had spent my whole life being the new kid.

"And don't be discouraged if you don't make friends right away," Lynn continued. "Some things take time."

Lynn hugged me so much I almost missed the school bus. I'd never ridden a school bus before. I sat toward the back next to a window so I could look out. I could feel eyes on me. Probably everyone on the bus, including the driver, was looking at me.

I knew Otis Crump was probably on the bus, but I wasn't going to look around. I wouldn't know which one he was anyway. I had no idea what he looked like. Mitch had called him an oversized oaf, so he must be big. Like that big ape Marvin Repler, I thought.

When the bus stopped at the school, I hurried off. I didn't look left or right. I just headed for the building and went straight to the office. Just like Lynn had told me to.

I couldn't believe the size of that school. Talk about dinky!

When I reached the office, I didn't see a secretary. There was just a tall, skinny guy sitting in a chair. His long legs were halfway across the desk. He was reading a newspaper.

I almost hollered, "Hey, you!" But then I remembered what Mrs. Bane had said about using good manners. I guessed I could give it a try. I'd never in my whole life called anybody "sir," and I wasn't about to start now. So I cleared my throat really hard and said, "Excuse me, where's the secretary?"

The man in the chair told me she was off sick. Then he asked if he could help me.

"My name is Patrick Engstrom," I said. "I moved here from Portland, and I live with Mitch and Lynn Kelly."

The man stood up. It took him forever, he was so tall. His face was just one solid grin.

"I'm supposed to give you these papers," I said. I laid them on the desk next to a nameplate that said ALLEN RYAN. "If you're the principal."

The man chuckled. "I'm the principal," he said. He stuck his hand out to shake hands with me. I'd never shaken hands before. I stuck my hand in his big paw. I threw my shoulders back and puffed my chest out a little.

"Welcome to our school, Patrick," Mr. Ryan said in a booming voice.

"Thank you, Mr. Ryan," I said while he pumped my hand.

I almost giggled. Boy, if Lynn and Mrs. Bane could see me now. Wasn't I the proper little gentleman?

I finally got things taken care of in the office. The class had already started when I got to my classroom. The fifth and sixth grades were together. The teacher's name was Mrs. Fletcher.

"Class, this is Patrick Engstrom," Mrs. Fletcher announced. "He comes to us from Portland. Let's make him feel welcome."

A lot of the kids smiled. One waved. The others stared. I took the desk Mrs. Fletcher pointed to and started counting the kids. There were only 19 kids in two grades!

Then I saw a boy sitting in the desk in the corner. He wasn't far from the teacher's desk. He had to be Otis Crump.

By the end of the week, the kids had gotten used to me. They finally stopped staring. I was really dreading the day I'd have to stand up and read in front of the class.

One night after dinner, I spread my books and stuff out on the table and started to do my homework. I hadn't forgotten what Mrs. Bane had said about doing my best. Well, my best was terrible.

Mitch had gone to some kind of meeting. I thought Lynn was watching something on television. But the next thing I knew, she was standing behind me looking over my shoulder.

I was trying to do a problem in my reading workbook. What did the paragraph tell me about the main character? It was multiple choice. All I had to do was take a chance and mark one of the three answers. But if I marked the wrong one, I could end up sounding dumb.

How the heck did I know what the paragraph told me? I only knew half the words in it. I had already erased most of my answers so many times the page was full of holes.

Lynn grabbed my hand. "Just a minute, Pat," she said. "How about reading this paragraph out loud. Maybe between the two of us we can figure it out."

I did a lot of stalling and stammering. What would Lynn do when she found out I couldn't read any better than a first grader?

Lynn pulled out a chair and sat down next to me. "Okay," she said. She held the book so we could both see it. I stumbled over a dozen words before Lynn spoke. "Looks like you could use a little help," she said as calm as could be.

I couldn't believe it! She wasn't the least bit shocked.

"There are a few tricks in learning to read, Pat," Lynn said. She smiled at me. "And you are about to learn them."

That was the beginning of the end of my dumbness. Lynn spent at least an hour with me every day after school. And she spent about three or four hours reading with me on weekends. And the crazy part about it was that I didn't mind. To tell the truth, I liked it a lot. I was really learning to read! Lynn said if you could read, you could learn anything.

Lynn and I went to town and checked out books at the library. We took turns reading them out loud. Until then, I hadn't known how neat books were.

But the neatest thing of all was the day I got an A in spelling. I had never gotten an A—or anything close to it—in my whole life. There were only ten words, but I spelled every one without erasing once.

I thought Lynn was going to break every bone in my body the way she hugged me. But I had to admit, I kind of liked it.

Even Mitch got a little crazy. He picked me clear off the floor and spun me around. "That's my buddy!" he yelled. "I wouldn't be surprised if you grew up to be president."

I felt like a nut. It was great!

7

The Skunk

I didn't really get to know Otis at school. But I
learned a lot about him just being in the same room
with him. And watching him on the playground. He
mostly hung out with the eighth-grade boys. There
were only three of them. Otis was 14 years old and
only in the sixth grade. And I thought I was dumb!

Mrs. Fletcher had to get on him about something every day. One day she sent him to the boys' rest room to wash his face and comb his hair. It didn't even embarrass him. He was a real slob.

I hadn't been back in the woods since that first day with Mitch. The weather had been pretty bad.

I'd been kind of tied up with school too. Though I hadn't really made any close friends, I hadn't made any enemies either.

This one Saturday was extra nice for the time of the year. The sun was shining, and it was a little bit warm. I begged off going to town shopping with Mitch and Lynn. The trip sounded okay, and I usually liked going with them. But I hated to waste such a nice day.

Lynn began to insist that I go. But Mitch came to my rescue. "He's old enough to stay alone," he said. "What could possibly happen?"

Lynn tried to tell him, but Mitch started pushing her toward the front door.

It was sort of a nice feeling having the whole place to myself. I thought about enjoying the privacy by just loafing around, maybe reading or watching cartoons on TV. But it was such a pretty day I decided against spending it in the house.

Then I had a great idea. I'd take Shorty out for a walk. But Shorty had different ideas. I tried standing him on his feet.

"Come on, Shorty," I pleaded. "Don't you want to go outside and take a walk?"

He didn't.

"At least open your eyes, Shorty. Okay?"

He wouldn't.

After about ten minutes, I gave up and pushed him back into his basket. If Shorty hadn't snored in his sleep, it would have been hard to tell if he was alive. Oh, well, I thought. He's old and tired.

I put a couple of apples in my jacket pocket and took off for the woods. I went farther than that time with Mitch. I walked clear to the back fence. I saw that the fence was down in a couple of places. I'd have to remember to tell Mitch when he got home. I'd even help him fix it. It sounded like fun.

Man, it was a great day! I sat down on a fallen log where the sun could hit my back. Then I ate one of the apples.

Was it ever quiet! The only sound was the slight rustling of limbs overhead from the little bit of breeze. I decided the country was pretty nice.

I soaked up the sun for a while. When I drew back my arm to throw the apple core away, something caught my eye. It was right by a little clump of bushes, not far from the fence. I could make out a little patch of white. I think I knew right away that it was an animal. And it was in a trap.

I stood up and started slowly walking toward it. When I got close, I saw the swollen, torn foot inside the steel jaws. It was covered with dried blood. I gagged, and the apple almost came up.

If you took all the times I'd been mad and put them all together, it wouldn't have been half the anger I was feeling right then. I'd kill him! The next time I saw that Otis Crump, I'd just walk up to him and kill him. I wasn't sure how, but I'd do it. I'd never, never, never hated anyone so much!

At first, I thought the little animal was dead. But when I knelt down beside it, I saw a slight movement. Like it was trying to get away. It was too weak to do anything but lie there. I knew it was a skunk, even though I'd never seen a real one before.

I put my face down closer. Its eyes opened, just barely. It was so awful. I could tell by its eyes that it was terrified. I knew I had to open the jaws of the trap. I only hoped I could do it.

"Hi, little skunk," I whispered. I was so choked up I couldn't talk out loud. I reached out slowly and put my hand on its fur. "I'm going to see if I can help you. Okay?"

I felt its heart beating faintly under my hand. I rubbed my hand along its body and whispered over and over. "It's going to be all right. It's going to be all right."

Suddenly, I felt its body relax some. Just like it knew I was trying to help. My eyes were burning like fire from the tears that wouldn't stay back. I hadn't cried for a long time. But I knelt there beside that poor little animal and blubbered like a baby. In my whole life—just like that—I'd never loved anything like I loved that nearly dead skunk.

Finally, I wiped my eyes on the back of my hand. I took as deep a breath as my dry throat would let me. Then, using my foot like Mitch showed me, I pried open the jaws of the trap. The skunk just lay there like it didn't even know it was free. I got a really good look at its foot. It was a mess. A little bit of fresh blood dribbled out of the gash.

A blast of anger went through me and almost took the top of my head off. I jerked the trap loose from where it was staked in the ground. And I started beating it against a tree, just like Mitch had. Then I threw it as hard as I could over the fence.

I knelt down by the little skunk. "Poor little thing," I murmured. I stroked its fur. It was so thin. I wondered how long it had been in that trap. With nothing to eat or drink. And half going out of its mind with pain and fear.

My mind was so full of hating Otis Crump I was getting a headache.

I kept rubbing the little skunk and talking to it. And its little black eyes never turned from my face.

"Nothing is ever going to hurt you again," I promised. "Not ever. I'm taking care of you. You're going to be mine. My very own." I thought that was the best sound I'd ever heard—"my very own." The feeling inside me was just about smothering me. But it still felt good.

I took off my jacket and spread it out on the ground. Carefully, I lifted the skunk onto my jacket and wrapped it up. It never dawned on me for a second that messing with a wild animal could be dangerous. That it could bite my hand off. And as for that other thing that skunks did, I never thought about that either.

I picked up the bundle and held it against my chest. I couldn't believe how light it was. The skunk gave a couple of little jerks, then lay still.

All the while, I talked to it. "Poor little skunk." It sounded silly calling it "little skunk." It had to have a name. "I'll think of a name for you," I said. "I'll think of a good name."

About that time, I tripped on a rock or something and almost fell. A faint squeak came from inside the jacket. A scared little squeak. I held the skunk close. Before I realized what I was saying, it popped out. "There, there, honey. You're all right, honey."

Hey! I thought excitedly. That's it! Honey!

Man! I'd never called anything or anybody "honey." Never. And here I was calling a skunk "Honey."

When I got to the house, I saw that Mitch and Lynn were still gone. I laid Honey on the kitchen table and turned the jacket back. Right away, the scared look came back. I started talking softly. "I won't hurt you," I said. "I wouldn't hurt you for anything." I stroked Honey's fur until her eyes closed.

I'd heard somewhere once that an animal or a person could go longer without food than water. I'd seen some eyedroppers in the medicine chest. "I'll be right back, Honey."

There was some peroxide in the medicine chest too. I'd seen Lynn put it on Toby's sores after he'd been in a cat fight. I took the bottle and some cotton balls and the eyedropper back to the kitchen.

Honey hadn't moved. Her eyes were closed. I poured some of the peroxide on a cotton ball and dabbed it on the open gash. Honey never made a move. I touched her. Her body felt different—not as soft as before. What was wrong? I started to get scared.

"Don't be d-dead," I stammered. "Please, Honey. Don't b-be dead."

I rushed to the sink and filled the dropper with water. I pushed it between Honey's lips and squeezed slowly. The water ran down her fur and onto the jacket. I could feel sweat on my forehead. I squeezed some more water into her mouth. It ran out too. My hands were shaking so much I could hardly hold on to the dropper. Honey's eyes stayed closed. I couldn't see any signs of life.

I didn't remember asking God for anything before. But it came to me that this might be a good time to start.

"Dear God," I prayed. "Could you do me a favor just this once? Could you make this little skunk be okay? It didn't do anything. It was all on account of that Otis Crump. That dirty . . ." I caught myself in time. "Please don't let her die. If you'll help me save her, I promise to take good care of her. Amen, God." I thought of something else. "P.S., God. Please do something awful to Otis Crump."

I filled the dropper with water again. The water kept running down the side of Honey's face. I started to panic. I pushed the dropper farther into her mouth, through her teeth. I closed my eyes and squeezed.

After what seemed like an hour, I heard a little sound—like a cough. I opened my eyes. The skunk was swallowing! Honey was swallowing the water! Again I filled the dropper. Honey swallowed every bit of it. I was laughing and crying all at once. It was crazy.

I took some milk out of the refrigerator. I filled the dropper twice. Honey swallowed all of it. Then she closed her eyes. But this time, I wasn't scared. I knew

Honey was tired and weak and needed to rest.

It felt really great knowing I had helped her. I had no idea how long she had been in the trap without food and water. I just hoped that I'd come along in time.

I dabbed a little more peroxide on Honey's foot. Then I sat down on a chair and waited for Mitch and Lynn. I could hardly wait to tell them how I'd taken the injured animal out of the trap all by myself.

At last I heard the car pull into the driveway. I held my breath as Lynn and Mitch walked into the kitchen. I was so proud of myself.

Lynn took one look at the skunk sleeping on the table and let out a blood-curdling scream. Mitch banged a sack of groceries down on the counter and shouted at me, "Good Lord, Pat! What is this?"

"It-it-it's a skunk," I stammered.

"I can see that!" he yelled. I didn't know Mitch could be so awful. "I want to know what in the world it's doing in this house!"

"And on the table!" Lynn added. "Oh, Pat. How could you?"

"It-it was in a trap, Mitch," I said. My throat was drying up on me. I was having trouble talking. "I thought it was dead at first. I took it out of the trap all by-by myself. I-I brought it in so I could take care of it."

The skunk's eyes had opened and were darting back and forth. It began to struggle, but it couldn't get to its feet. I reached over to put my hand on it. "It-it's all right, Honey." I was having a hard time trying to keep from crying.

"Don't touch it, Pat!" Lynn yelled. "Oh, Mitch. Do something!"

Mitch took off into their bedroom. When he came back, he was carrying a gun. A .22 rifle.

"What are you going to do?" I screamed.

Mitch set the gun on the counter. He grabbed my shoulders and shook me until I stopped screaming. "Pat, listen to me." He wasn't shouting now. "This animal is almost dead. The kindest thing to do would be to put it out of its misery."

"No," I sobbed. "It's mine."

"It's a young female, I think," Mitch said. "Even if her life could be saved—which it can't—you couldn't keep her. She wouldn't belong to you."

"But she does," I insisted. "She's mine."

"Pat, it's a wild animal," Mitch explained. "A skunk can be very dangerous. They can carry rabies. You're just lucky you didn't get bitten, or at least sprayed."

"But she didn't hurt me," I reasoned. "She knew I was trying to help her."

Mitch picked up the gun. "I'm sorry, Pat. I really am."

"Sure you are!" I snapped. 'I'll just bet you are!"

I whirled around to face Lynn. "You're just like all the rest—both of you! You don't want me to have anything but what you pick! I hate you!"

Before either one of them could say anything, I grabbed up the jacket and Honey and tore out the back door. I ran as fast as my legs would carry me.

When I looked back over my shoulder, I was surprised to find that Mitch was not following me. He and Lynn were standing side by side on the back porch, just watching me.

I didn't slow down, though. When I finally did stop, I wasn't even sure where I was. But I knew I was far away, and that was all that mattered. I sat down on the ground and leaned against a tree. I thought I'd never catch my breath. My lungs hurt.

I spread the jacket out on my lap. Honey's eyes were open. She looked all upset. I tried to calm her down, but I was panting so hard I could hardly talk.

"There, there now, Honey." I rubbed her fur. "It's all right. I-I won't let him kill you. I promise."

I scooted all the way down until I was lying on the ground. I cradled Honey on my arm. I talked to her until I knew she was not afraid anymore. After a long time, we both fell asleep.

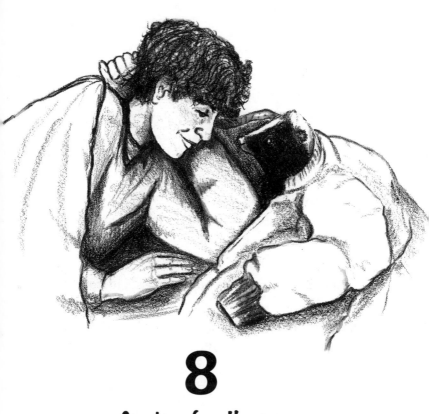

8

Caring for Honey

I guess it was the cold that woke me up. I didn't know how long I'd slept. But I felt kind of groggy. Maybe because of the dreams. It took me a little while to realize they were dreams and not things that had really happened.

I dreamed that I'd knocked Otis Crump down and socked him in the face over and over. I'd socked him until my knuckles were so sore I could hardly move my hands.

I had another dream too. Mitch was whipping me something awful and yelling. "You knew better! I'll teach you never to do anything like that again!" Mitch yelled in my dream.

Then Lynn started pulling him away and screaming. "You leave him alone! Don't hurt him!" She was crying. "Don't hurt my baby!"

What a dumb dream, I thought.

But lying there, looking up at the sky, it didn't seem right. I closed my eyes tight. I could do that sometimes if my dreams were all fuzzy, and it would clear them up. Sure, something was wrong. It wasn't Mitch that was beating me. It was Rick. It was because I'd wet myself. And the dream was so real I reached down and felt to make sure it hadn't really happened.

And it wasn't Lynn that was crying, "Don't hurt my baby!" It was *her*.

"Ha!" I sneered right out loud. That would be the day. A lot *she* ever cared what happened to me.

She had no business getting into my dreams. She could just stay at that funny farm until she died, as far as I was concerned. She probably didn't even remember me anyway, with her mind all messed up the way it was.

I blinked hard and turned over. I was face to face with Honey. Her eyes were open, and she was staring at me. She looked so cute and curious, like she was wondering what the heck was going on. I giggled. "Hi there, Honey."

Honey's eyes got bigger and rounder. Her nose twitched. "You want to smell me, huh?" I said.

I put out my hand slowly. Then her nose really twitched.

"Guess what, Honey," I said. "I love you."

I didn't even feel dumb saying it. I had this real puffed-up feeling in my chest. But I had this other feeling too. Like a bitter taste in my mouth. From something I'd said to Mitch and Lynn. I didn't mean it about hating them.

But Mitch had no right to kill Honey without even giving her a chance. I could kind of understand Lynn acting the way she did. I guess putting Honey on the table hadn't been such a good idea.

I put my hand on Honey's fur and rubbed her. She was so soft and cute. How could anybody not love her? Especially after the awful thing that had happened to her.

"Know something, Honey?" I said to her. "I know just what it's like. I bet if I'd been born an animal, I'd have been a skunk."

I knew I had to get more food and water down her soon. Water wasn't too much of a problem. I could always find a puddle. But what would I get it in? I hadn't thought of that. I wished I had brought the dropper with me.

Honey wasn't even trying to get up, so I knew she was still very weak. If I carried her to a puddle she probably wouldn't be able to drink by herself.

As for food, I didn't have the slightest idea what skunks ate. But I had to find something for her to eat or she'd die.

I was getting pretty hungry myself. I hadn't had anything to eat since the apple that morning. The apple! I had put two in my pocket, and I'd only eaten one. I found the other one in my pocket and took a big bite out of it. I hoped skunks liked apples. I chewed for a long time until I got it all mushy and wet. I picked up a little stick about six inches long. Using my pocketknife, I cut the end of the stick to make it flat— as much like a spoon as I could.

I spit some of the juicy pulp on the stick and pushed it inside Honey's mouth. I thought she was going to eat the stick and all. She was chewing! Not fast, but she was chewing and making gurgling noises.

I got about a fourth of the apple down her before she got tired and closed her eyes. I felt so good about getting her to eat, I forgot about being hungry myself.

I put the rest of the apple back in my pocket for when she woke up again. I figured the juice in the apple would be as good as water—for now anyway.

While Honey slept, I got up and moved around a little. It was getting cold. I had my jacket, but I needed that for Honey's bed. I looked around to see if there was a shed or a building of some kind that we could stay in. I couldn't see any. I knew I had to figure out something pretty soon.

If I had some money, I could take Honey to a vet, I thought. He could doctor her foot and give her something to get her strength back. But where in the heck was I going to get any money?

I did a lot of thinking, but I didn't solve anything. It was a cinch I'd have to split now. But how was I going to make it? It was hard enough alone, but now I had Honey to think about.

Honey woke up, and I fed her again. I ripped a piece of my shirttail off and dipped it in a puddle. When I squeezed the water into Honey's mouth, some of it ran down her face. But she swallowed a lot of it. I squeezed some water on her sore foot too.

It started getting dark. My stomach was so empty it had sharp pains shooting through it. I spread the jacket out flat and worked Honey, back end first, down in one of the sleeves. All that was sticking out was her funny, cute little face.

71

Her dark, round eyes really watched me. I had to laugh every time she looked at me that way. I knew if she could talk she'd be asking a lot of questions. I scooted up as close to her as I could get and covered myself with the rest of the jacket. It was a little warmer, but not much.

I watched the sky grow darker. I put my arm over my ear to shut out the night noises. When an owl hooted, I nearly jumped out of my skin. I ached all over, and a rock was poking my ribs.

I'll never be able to sleep, I thought. But I did. It didn't seem like I'd been asleep very long before the sun woke me up. It was shining right in my face. I opened my eyes, but I had to close them instantly. It was so bright.

I heard a voice. "Pat! Hey, Pat!" someone called.

I opened my eyes again and pulled myself up on my elbow. It wasn't the sun shining in my face—it was still pitch dark. It was a flashlight, and Mitch was coming toward me calling my name.

I sprang to my feet ready to grab the jacket with Honey in it. But Mitch grabbed me before I could make a move.

"You let me go!" I yelled. "You're not going to kill her!" I kicked him in the shins. "Let me go! You've got no right to kill her."

I slugged Mitch with both fists as hard as I could. But he still held on.

"Listen to me, Pat," Mitch pleaded. "Please listen to me."

When I'd fought him until I couldn't fight anymore, I broke down and cried. I couldn't help myself. Mitch held me in his arms and pushed my head down on his shoulder. He waited until I'd cried myself out. Then he handed me his handkerchief.

"You okay now, son?" he whispered against my ear.

My voice was all jerky with sobs. "I-I-won't-let you kill-her," I blubbered.

"I'm not going to kill her, Pat," Mitch said. "If she means this much to you, we'll try to save her."

We! He said *we!* I couldn't believe it! I could have hugged him. I could have thrown my arms around his neck and hugged him. I would have too, I thought. But just then, Mitch picked up the flashlight from where he'd dropped it on the ground and shined it on Honey.

"How's she doing?" Mitch asked.

"I think she's a little better," I said.

"I can't believe she hasn't sprayed you," Mitch said. "It doesn't make sense."

It made sense to me. Why would she want to hurt someone who was trying to help her? She knew I was her friend.

"Pat," Mitch said. "I'm not going to pretend I like this idea. Like I said before, wild animals can be dangerous. They carry diseases. They can turn on you at any time."

"Honey won't," I insisted. "She's just as safe as anything."

Mitch laughed. "You'll change your mind the first time she gets upset or frightened. Wait till you get a whiff of it."

It seemed to me Honey would have done it by then if she was going to. She'd already been upset and frightened. And even if she did, there had to be worse things in the world than bad smells.

On the way back to the house, Mitch told me he'd fixed up an old rabbit hutch for Honey.

"But I want her close to me," I protested. "I want to be able to keep an eye on her."

"I know you do, Pat," Mitch said. "But animals—especially wild ones—do better all alone when they're sick or hurt. At least part of the time. She'll be right out the back door. I'm afraid it's going to be up to you to feed her," he laughed. "There's no way you're going to get Lynn or me that close to her."

The hutch Mitch had fixed up for her was really neat. There was a little box filled with bedding that she could get into. Inside it was dark and quiet.

Before I put her in the box inside the hutch, I doctored her foot with some salve that Lynn gave me. I got some more water down her. And some canned dog food thinned down with milk and cod liver oil.

Mitch wouldn't let me feed her as much as I

wanted. "It will do her more harm than good," he explained. "She'll have to have small meals more often until she can eat by herself."

"But how can I feed her if I have to go to school?" I asked.

"No problem," Lynn said.

Until Honey was able to eat by herself, Lynn said she'd drive to school and bring me home during lunch. Then I could take care of her.

"Lynn-Mitch," I stammered. It wasn't easy. I'd never done much apologizing in my life. "I-I'm sorry I-I said I hated you. I didn't mean it."

Lynn and Mitch each put an arm around me, and we walked into the house.

I ate three bowls of stew—carrots and all—four muffins, half a jar of peaches, and two cups of hot chocolate. Boy, did I ever sleep that night.

9

Learning to Trust

I checked on Honey Monday morning. It was hard to believe she was the same little skunk I had taken out of the trap.

I'd fed Honey and doctored her foot several times Sunday. Each time, her foot looked better, and she ate a little more. Lynn chopped up some raw liver until it was all bloody and soupy. I gagged the entire time Honey was eating it. But I'd swear she was smacking her lips.

Mitch made me let Honey rest as much as possible. It wasn't easy. I could have spent every minute with her.

Mitch and I fixed the fence and did a few chores around the place. It was hard work, but it was fun.

Mitch watched me feed Honey Monday morning before he went to work. "I would have bet money that she would have been dead long before this," he said.

"I'm a good doctor," I boasted, grinning at Mitch.

Mitch smiled back at me and ruffled my hair. "It was a lot more than doctoring that saved that animal's life, Pat," he said.

I knew what Mitch meant. He was right too. I sure was crazy about that little skunk. I'd never had a pet of my own before. And I'd certainly never dreamed that I would ever have a pet skunk.

Mitch told me that there was a law against keeping a wild animal—except under certain conditions. As soon as Honey was better, we were going to see about getting a permit from the Oregon Department of Fish and Wildlife. Mitch said he was sure it would be no problem. We would have to take her to a vet to get shots and have her descented.

I'd given myself a long lecture that morning when I first woke up. About not killing Otis Crump. I was not going to start anything at school or on the bus. Even though I was just plain sick to my stomach with hatred for him. But things were going smooth for me. No way was I going to blow it. And I figured I owed Mitch and Lynn more than that. I wouldn't shame them.

Otis got on the bus at the same stop as me. I was just ahead of him. Some other kids were going up the bus steps. He gave me a shove from behind. "Get a move on, kid," he said. Then he giggled that dumb, idiotic giggle of his.

I whirled around with both fists clenched. It was a reflex. I whirled around so fast I made Otis lose his balance. He stumbled back to the ground. His face was just about level with my foot. If I'd kicked him, my foot would have caught him right in his big mouth.

It was a good thing that the bus driver said, "Hey, you kids quit clowning around and get on the bus. I've got a schedule to meet."

That bus driver didn't know it, but he did Otis and me a big favor. At least he postponed things for a while.

I stomped to the back of the bus and sat down. I spent the whole ride glaring at the back of Otis's head. I kept seeing Honey—her little foot caught in that trap. She was hurt and terrified, struggling to get free. Mitch said that animals had been known to actually chew off their own feet trying to get out of a trap.

There ought to be a law! But there wasn't. Oh, sure. They had laws that said you couldn't trap without a license. You couldn't set traps on private property. You had to check your traps by a certain length of time. But what good was that? It didn't help the animals any. I figured anyone who was low enough to trap sure as heck wasn't going to pay any attention to laws anyway.

By the time I got to school, I'd calmed down a little. I'd have to stay away from Otis Crump—until the right time.

Lynn picked me up at lunch time. She told me she'd looked out the window at Honey's box about every half hour. But she hadn't seen any movement at all.

But before I was out the door with her lunch, Honey's nose was poking out the opening of her box. She knew me! She sniffed my hand for a long time after she finished eating.

We had a study period in the library that afternoon. I found some books about skunks and read them. I learned some really interesting things. Honey was a striped skunk, and there were thirteen species of her kind. Her Latin name was—I couldn't even pronounce it—*Mephitis*. It meant "bad odor."

So far, that wasn't Honey. She had a little bit of a funny smell, but it wasn't really bad. In fact, old Shorty smelled a whole lot worse than Honey did.

The stuff skunks spray out was called musk. It comes out of two glands under their tails. They could shoot the musk about twelve feet. It wasn't poison, but it could burn eyes really bad because it had sulfuric acid in it.

I thought it was neat that when they get excited or upset, they stamp their front feet as fast as they can. Like beating a drum.

I was looking at a picture of a skunk in one of the books. I was thinking how cute it was and how much it looked like Honey. Then the girl sitting next to me said, "Yuck! What are you reading?"

"It happens to be a book about skunks," I made myself answer.

"Yes, but why are you reading about them?" the girl asked. "Skunks are smelly."

"So are some people I know," I snapped at her. She didn't even notice.

I turned the page and started reading again. There was a picture of a baby skunk inside a cowboy boot. All that was sticking out was its head and front feet.

"Oooh!" the girl gushed in my ear. "Look at that. Isn't it cute?"

I gave her my most surprised look. She really meant it! When I looked at her that time, I noticed something I hadn't noticed before. She was pretty cute herself.

"It says here that skunks make good pets," she said. She'd scooted so close her hair was tickling my nose.

"They do," I said. "I have—" I caught myself in time. "I mean I know a kid who has one." I didn't figure it was a good idea to say anything about Honey yet.

"Really?" She was impressed. "Doesn't it stink?"

I told her all I knew about skunks. Then we read the books together. Her name was Holly. Kind of a nice name, I thought.

At the dinner table that night, I told Mitch and Lynn everything I'd found out about skunks. The books said skunks could be trained to use a litter box and be led on a leash. They said skunks could be fed a lot of different things—meat, canned dog food, fruit, and vegetables. But they shouldn't have very many sweets.

There was something else in the books. Something that really bothered me. Baby skunks could be descented with no problems. But after they were about six months old, the operation could be serious—sometimes fatal. I was sure Mitch didn't know that. All he'd said was that after they'd been descented they had no way of defending themselves against danger. I didn't tell Lynn and Mitch everything I'd read.

By the time I'd had Honey a month, she was just about back to normal. Her foot was a little bit crooked, but she could stamp it right along with the other one whenever she got excited or scared. Like whenever she saw Toby or Shorty. And once when a hawk swooped down in the yard after a mouse.

But Honey never sprayed—not once. I could take her out of the hutch and go for walks with her sitting on my shoulder.

"You've got to have more nerve than good sense, Pat," Mitch said. "To put a skunk that close to your face."

I guess I didn't have much sense when it came to Honey. I just figured as long as she trusted me, everything was okay. She never tried to run away when I set her on the ground. If she did wander very far from me, I could coax her back. I'd hold out a cracker or some other kind of food and call her name. I loved that little skunk more every day.

Mitch seemed to have forgotten about getting the permit and taking her to the vet for the operation. I sure wasn't going to remind him.

10

Worst Days

I'd always known that the day would come when I'd have to tangle with Otis. But I sure didn't know that I'd almost get myself killed when it happened.

I still remembered the great feeling I'd had when I'd clobbered Marvin Repler. After he'd teased me into blowing my cool. I guess I was still pretty sure of myself. Maybe that's why I was positive I could beat him to a bloody pulp. I jumped Otis on the school playground, after I'd promised myself it wouldn't happen at school.

It was because of what had happened to Honey that I hated Otis so much. The odd part was that it was something else that made me fight him. But as far as I was concerned, it was for Honey.

It was during afternoon recess. I was playing catch with a kid named Dale. I'd thrown the ball, and Otis, giggling like an idiot as usual, ran between us and caught it. Before I could even finish yelling, "Hey, knock it off!" he threw the ball on the ground and took off.

A couple of minutes later, Otis was back. This time when he caught the ball and ran, he smacked right into a girl and pushed her down. It was a little girl—a second grader. He didn't help her up or say he was sorry. He just stood there pointing his grimy finger at her and braying like a donkey. I saw red!

"You big creep!" I screamed at the top of my lungs. I was spitting like crazy.

Dale tried to grab my arm as I lunged at Otis, but I jerked away from him. When Otis laughed, slobber bubbled out of his mouth and ran down his chin. The last thing I remember was Otis's slobbery grin and a fist the size of a cannonball coming at my face.

There was a cot in the little room next to the office. That's where I was when I realized what had happened. The light on the ceiling was spinning like a top. So was my head. Mr. Ryan and Lynn were standing over me.

"Pat," Lynn said with a catch in her voice. "Are you okay?"

Before I could answer, she cried, "You scared us half to death!"

I opened my mouth to tell her I was all right. Blood ran in. When I sat up, gagging, I found the blood was coming from my nose.

The first thing that popped into my mind was that I'd probably be kicked out of school. If that happened, all of Mrs. Bane's troubles would have been for nothing. It was either Woodlawn or running away, hoping I could make it on my own.

I didn't have to spend much time worrying about it. Mr. Ryan sat down by the cot. He told me what a nice thing I'd done for the little girl.

I know I must have gasped. I never thought the time would come when I'd get praised for fighting. Mr. Ryan went on to say how Otis was nothing but trouble and always had been. It turned out Otis was the one who got kicked out of school—for the rest of the week anyway.

"By the way, Pat," Mr. Ryan said. "You got in a couple of good licks yourself. Otis has a split lip that may require a stitch. Some of the kids said you flew at him so hard you butted him in the face with your head."

I tried to grin, but it hurt. "So that's why I've got this headache?"

I had more than a headache. I had a black eye that was swollen shut and a knot on my head the size of a golf ball. Somehow, I had even twisted my ankle.

With Otis out of the way, I thought my troubles were over. But I was wrong.

The worst day of my life came one week later. The first thing I saw when I got off the bus was Mrs. Bane's car parked in the driveway. I had been excited because I had something special to show Lynn. A history paper with only one wrong answer and "very good" written across the top. Now I could show Mrs. Bane too. I could imagine her surprise. I hoped she wouldn't faint.

I came skidding to a stop in the living room where Mrs. Bane was sitting on the couch with Lynn. I could tell they had both been crying.

"Hello, Pat," Mrs. Bane whispered. Then she motioned me to sit by her on the couch. My shoes felt like they were full of lead as I shuffled toward her. "I'm afraid I-I-have some-some bad news for you, Pat."

Mrs. Bane was squeezing my arm so tight it hurt. My heart had jumped up in my throat and was stuck there. Mrs. Bane sobbed a little.

"It's—it's your mother—" Mrs. Bane began.

She didn't have to tell me any more. I knew. I swallowed around the lump in my throat. I could only whisper. "She's—my mother is—is dead, isn't she?"

Mrs. Bane just squeezed my arm tighter. Lynn bawled right out loud.

"Did she—you know—do it? Did she—" I couldn't make myself say the words.

Mrs. Bane nodded and wiped her eyes.

I felt cold and sweaty all over. How could she? How could she do that?

"She did it because of me, didn't she?" I was screaming and I couldn't stop. "Because she was afraid they'd make her leave someday, and then she'd have to take care of me!"

Through the pounding in my head, I heard Mrs. Bane say, "She did it because she couldn't help herself, Pat. Because she was ill. Very, very ill." Mrs. Bane pushed something into my hand. "This is for you, Pat. It was in her hand when they—they found her."

It was an envelope with my name printed on it. I could feel what was in it before I opened it. Ever since I could remember, she'd worn a locket that she said her mother had given her before she'd died. There was a picture in it. It was my mother holding me when I was a baby.

My hands were shaking so hard I could hardly take it out of the envelope. It was wrapped in a piece of notepaper. The writing was so faint and scribbly, I had a hard time reading it.

Dear Patrick, this is for you, honey. Please remember me. I am so sorry. Love, Mom.

I wadded up the paper and shoved it in my pocket with the locket.

"I have to go feed Honey," I said hurriedly.

I had to get out of there quickly. I grabbed a couple of crackers as I went through the kitchen. I put Honey up on my shoulder. When I got to the woods I sat down and gave Honey the crackers.

Well, she wouldn't have to worry about getting stuck with me again, I thought. Not ever again. I pulled the note out of my pocket and smoothed it out. I read it again out loud. The words rang in my ears. "I'm so sorry. I'm so sorry. I'm so sorry."

I threw myself face down on the ground and cried. I cried for my mother because I missed her. I did love her—I did! And I knew she had loved me the best she could.

When I finally stopped crying and turned over, Honey was watching me with round, curious eyes. I put her on my shoulder and headed back to the house.

Mrs. Bane was gone. I was sorry. I'd write to her. I'd tell her all about school and Honey and how much I liked being with Mitch and Lynn. And I'd tell her I understood about my mother.

I might even thank her for all she'd done for me.

11

Good Days at Last

That was the worst day of my life. But it was
followed by a lot of good days. Good days at school,
where I was finally beginning to make friends. Good
days with Lynn and Mitch doing fun things. And
learning what it was like to be wanted and cared for.
Good days with Honey watching her grow stronger day
by day. Knowing that she loved me and trusted me.

Then there was an especially good day. We all got dressed up in our best clothes.

"For a special occasion," Mitch said. "Very, very special."

Mitch was wearing a suit with a tie and everything. Lynn was wearing a fancy dress trimmed with some lacy stuff. It was a maternity dress, but it still barely fit her.

We went all the way to Salem to a big, swanky restaurant. I nearly choked on my water when I got a look at the dinner prices.

It was the best meal I'd ever eaten. But I was glad when I finished. I was going crazy wondering what the special occasion was.

I emptied the dish of mints on the table while Lynn and Mitch drank their after-dinner coffee. When I couldn't wait any longer, I said, "Well?"

"Well what?" Lynn asked. She pretended she didn't know what I was talking about.

I grinned. I felt a little dumb being so impatient. But I had to know.

"The big occasion," I said. "The big surprise. You got me something special, right?"

Mitch gave an exaggerated gasp. "Did you hear that?" he said to Lynn. "Something special for *him!*"

Lynn made clicking noises with her tongue. "Aren't you ashamed, Pat?" she said, like I was about five years old. "Thinking that the special something had to be for you?"

I was embarrassed. I had jumped to conclusions—thinking it had to be something for me.

So it must be something else. Like maybe Mitch got a raise or a new job. Or maybe Lynn won one of those contests she was always entering.

Lynn started laughing. "Tell him, Mitch."

Mitch laughed too. "We're celebrating becoming parents," he said.

I shook my head and blinked. "But—but that's no surprise," I said.

Mitch was grinning all over his face. He reached into his jacket pocket and took out an envelope. He handed it to me.

"What's this?" I asked. I began taking some papers out of the envelope.

"Adoption papers," Mitch and Lynn said together.

"Adoption?" I mouthed. My tongue tied itself into a knot. I looked from Lynn to Mitch and then back. I could feel my mouth hanging open.

Mitch finally spoke. "Of course, if you'd rather not be adopted," he said in a teasing way.

It suddenly hit me smack in the brain. They wanted to adopt *me!* They wanted to be my mother and father!

"It will be a year before it's final," Lynn said. Her eyes were all teary. "But we couldn't wait to celebrate."

I giggled and sniffled and even hiccuped. Mitch and Lynn giggled and sniffled too. But they didn't hiccup.

We left the restaurant with our arms around each other. Everyone in the place was staring and smiling.

When we got back to Lebanon, we stopped for ice cream. Then we headed home. It was almost midnight, but no one was sleepy. So we talked for over an hour. I couldn't believe I wasn't dreaming.

Every few minutes, Lynn grabbed me and kissed me. I didn't even try to stop her. Lynn told me they had decided to adopt me the day Mrs. Bane came to tell me about my mother.

"We figured a kid with a name like Patrick would be perfect for a family named Kelly," Mitch said.

"Patrick Kelly," I said proudly. "Pat Kelly. Patrick Neal Kelly. It *does* sound all right."

"About as Irish as you can get," laughed Mitch.

Things just kept getting better and better after that. It was a great feeling being part of a family—a real part.

A couple of times I'd step out of line a little. But Mitch gave me heck just like I'd always been his kid. I didn't even mind it.

The nicer the weather got, the more I took Honey out. Sometimes we went to the woods. And sometimes in the field behind the house. Honey loved hunting for insects, and she was getting good at it.

I wondered what it was like for her being taken out in the daytime. Skunks are night animals. They hunt at night and usually sleep all day.

"You'll get used to it," I told Honey. She was riding on my shoulder the way she liked. I guess she could see better when we went for walks.

I took a piece of carrot out of my pocket and handed it to her.

Maybe that's not the real reason I wanted her to ride on my shoulder, I thought. Maybe it was because I was afraid she'd run away if I put her on the ground too often. But why would she want to run away? She loved me—I knew she did. And if it hadn't been for me . . .

All of a sudden, Honey started stamping her front feet as fast as she could on my shoulder. I caught her before she fell. Just as I set her on the ground, I saw what had upset her. It was Otis Crump! He was on his knees not 30 feet away. And he was setting a trap.

I bent down just as quietly as I could. Then I picked up a limb that was just the right size for what I had in mind. For splitting Otis Crump's head open.

I managed to get right behind him. He didn't hear a thing. I raised the limb high in the air, holding it tight with both hands. I yelled at the top of my lungs, *"You rotten scum!"*

It all happened so fast that I got dizzy. Otis jerked and fell forward. There was a dull thud followed by a blood-curdling scream. The scream was followed by the most gosh-awful smell I'd ever smelled in my life.

I thought I'd die laughing when I saw what had happened. There was Otis Crump with his hand caught in his own trap. And there was Honey prancing around with her tail high in the air. She was squirting that gook right in his face.

Even if I'd wanted to help that creep, I couldn't have. I couldn't stop laughing long enough to catch my breath. The harder Otis screamed, the harder I laughed.

But I knew that sooner or later Otis was going to get out of that trap. And as soon as his eyes stopped burning, he'd see who it was that had gotten him into such a fix. And then he was going to kill me.

I held out a piece of carrot, and Honey came to me. I held her with one hand and my nose with the other. I ran all the way home. Mitch and Lynn laughed as hard as I did when I told them all about it. But Lynn was worried.

"No telling what Otis will do if he catches you alone," Lynn said.

"If Otis didn't see Pat, how will he know who it was?" Mitch said. "Maybe he'll even think it was me."

Mitch was right. I hadn't thought about it. Otis didn't see me, I was sure of that. And he couldn't have known who that yell belonged to. It had sounded like something from another world. My throat was still hurting. And no one knew about Honey. I hadn't told a single person. I had been afraid I might get in trouble for keeping a wild animal without a license.

"It's a cinch he's not going to go around telling anyone about it," Mitch laughed. "I sure wouldn't if it happened to me. I think it's about time I had a talk with his father."

The last thing Mitch said to me that night before I went to bed was, "We'll have to get her in right away and have her descented. I'll try to get off a little early tomorrow. You be ready."

I didn't answer. I just nodded. I knew for sure that Mitch didn't know the operation could be dangerous.

I was awake for a long time that night. I loved that little skunk more than I'd ever loved anything in my life. And I knew she loved me. But deep down inside I knew she would never be as happy with me as she would be living free with her own kind. The way nature meant for her to. She was a wild animal. It wasn't right to try to make her anything else.

I got up before daylight the next morning. I stuffed my pockets full of food for Honey. All the things she liked. An apple, crackers, carrots, some hamburger, grapes, and a pretzel. I put a flashlight inside my belt and went out to Honey's cage.

Honey wasn't asleep. She was just crouched in a corner looking off toward the woods. I wondered if she was thinking about the excitement the day before. She still smelled awful. When she saw me, she got all happy and started begging for food. I gave her the pretzel.

I went farther than I'd ever gone before. Past our fence and on some land that was owned by a logging company. We finally got to an area that had been replanted a few years before. I decided this would be a good place for Honey to live.

I dumped all the food on the ground and set Honey down. She was like a little kid at Christmas trying to decide which toy to play with first. She'd pick up a grape. Then drop it when she spotted a cracker or a piece of apple.

I knew I had to get out of sight before she got through eating. And before I changed my mind. I put my hand on her back. "Good-bye, Honey," I sniffled. "I'm sure going to miss you."

It was the saddest thing I'd ever done. But I turned away and started running home. It was hard to see— my eyes were so full of tears.

When I got to our fence line, I looked back. But I couldn't see her.

"Have a good life, Honey!" I yelled.

I thought about Honey a lot. And I missed her even more than I thought I would. But Honey wasn't really gone. She was there in her cage begging for food every morning when I came out the door. She was sitting on my shoulder, sniffing in my ear every time I took a walk. Honey would never really be gone. She was part of my life forever. She'd taught me more than anyone would ever know.

Mitch said she might even show up at the back door begging for a handout someday. But for now, she had things that had to be taken care of. Like learning to be a skunk again and raising a family.

The week after I'd set Honey free my baby sister was born. Talk about excitement! Lynn's labor started about 3:00 in the morning. Mitch was tearing around the house like an idiot, gathering up stuff Lynn had to take to the hospital. I was glad when they finally left.

I went to school that morning and tried to pretend it was just another day. I couldn't concentrate on anything. Imagine *me* being a big brother, I thought. I felt ten feet tall.

When Mitch took me to see Lynn after school, she was in a mushy mood. She kept telling me how much she loved me. And how glad she was that I was going to be their son. Then she started gushing about the baby. "Oh, Pat! She's so cute! You're going to love her!"

I felt funny. I didn't know what I was supposed to

say. "What—what's her name?" I finally mumbled.

"Susan," Lynn answered.

"Oh, that's—that's pretty," I said. "What's her middle name?"

"We thought it would be nice if you chose her middle name," Lynn said.

I couldn't believe it! I thought for a minute. "How about Marie?" I asked.

"I love it," Lynn answered. "I really love it."

So did I. It was my mother's name.

About the Author

Bonnie Highsmith Taylor is a native Oregonian. She loves camping in the Oregon mountains and watching birds and other wildlife. Writing is Ms. Taylor's first love. But she also enjoys going to plays and concerts, collecting antique dolls, and listening to good music.